Holly Holiday

and the

CHRISTMAS FOREST

by **Katie Anderson** *Illustrated by* **Art Mawhinney**

GREENLEAF
BOOK GROUP PRESS

To my little Sugar Cookie, Ginger Snap, and Cinnamon Roll

This is Holly Holiday.

Holly Holiday LOVED Christmas!

She loved everything about it.

She loved the lights,

she loved the smells,

she loved the presents.

But more than anything,

she LOVED the Christmas tree.

She loved the way it filled her
house with anticipation and magic.

But the day after Christmas . . .

her parents dragged the tree out to the street.

"What are you *doing*?!" asked Holly.

"We're throwing away the tree," her parents replied.

"Throwing it *away*? *Why*?" asked Holly.

Her parents looked at each other and said, "It's dead."

"It's DEAD?!" exclaimed Holly.

Well, this just would not do for Holly Holiday.

"Magic doesn't end just like that. It needs to grow!"

Holly called a family meeting and shared her vision.

And the next year, instead of going to a tree lot . . .

Holly took her family to their local nursery

and selected a potted, living Christmas tree.

It was a bit smaller than Holly was used to,

but after she decorated it with lights and love . . .

it filled her house with more magic

than any tree had before.

And the day after Christmas,
instead of dragging a dead tree out to the street . . .

Holly and her family drove out into nature.

They found a beautiful sun-lit meadow . . .
and planted her living tree.

Year after year, Christmas after Christmas,
Holly would return to visit,

not just her Christmas tree—

but her Christmas forest.

Holly Holiday's Chocolate Chip Cookies

INGREDIENTS

1 ½ cup flour

½ tsp. salt

½ tsp. baking soda

½ cup (1 stick) butter softened

½ cup sugar

½ cup brown sugar

1 egg

1 tsp. vanilla extract

1 tsp. vanilla bean paste

1 bag chocolate chips

optional: ½ tsp. cinnamon

DIRECTIONS

1. With the supervision of an adult, preheat the oven to 375°F

2. Mix flour, salt, and baking soda in a bowl. Set aside.

3. In a new bowl, mix butter, sugar, and brown sugar together.

4. Add egg and vanilla extract and vanilla paste.

5. Add the dry flour mix to the wet batter mix.

6. Add bag of chocolate chips and cinnamon.

7. Line a cookie sheet with parchment paper.

8. Space dough balls three fingers apart.

9. Bake for 7 minutes.

10. Let cool and enjoy!

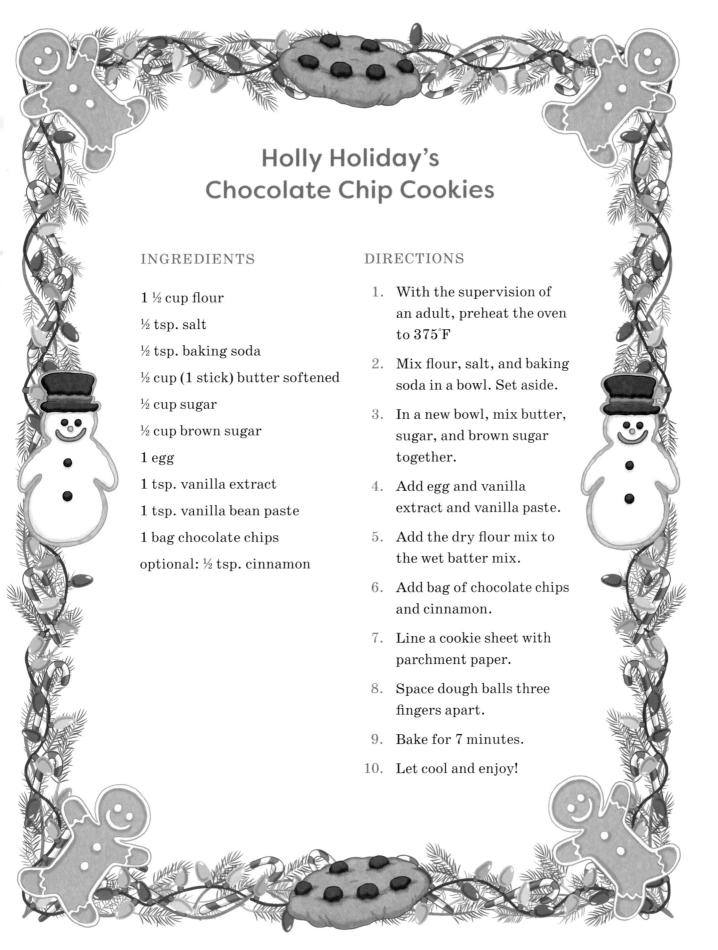

How to Plant a Tree

With the supervision and guidance of an adult, first find an empty space that will allow the roots and branches of the tree to spread.

Once you've found the perfect spot, dig a hole two times as wide and as deep as the tree's root ball.

Then, remove the tree from its container and place the root ball in the hole, making sure that the top of the root ball is at soil level.

Fill the hole with soil until it is level with the surrounding ground.

Gently step on the field soil to remove air pockets.

Water your tree well and cover the wet soil with mulch or dried leaves.

Katie Anderson
Writer

Katie Anderson found her love for storytelling while working as a camp counselor at Fallen Leaf Lake. She loves celebrating all holidays with her husband and three children. Together they keep the magic growing.

Art Mawhinney
Illustrator

Art Mawhinney studied art and animation, and has worked in the animation and illustration field for over 45 years. He has illustrated over 150 children's books.

Published by Greenleaf Book Group Press
Austin, Texas
www.gbgpress.com

Distributed by Greenleaf Book Group

For ordering information or special discounts for bulk purchases, please contact Greenleaf Book Group at PO Box 91869, Austin, TX 78709, 512.891.6100.

Design and composition by Greenleaf Book Group
Cover design by Greenleaf Book Group

Publisher's Cataloging-in-Publication data is available.

Print ISBN: 978-1-62634-956-8
eBook ISBN: 978-1-62634-957-5

Part of the Tree Neutral® program, which offsets the number of trees consumed in the production and printing of this book by taking proactive steps, such as planting trees in direct proportion to the number of trees used: www.treeneutral.com

Printed in Canada on acid-free paper

22 23 24 25 26 27   10 9 8 7 6 5 4 3 2 1

First Edition